STRANGE
MYSTERIES

Thomas G. Gunning

STRANGE MYSTERIES

Illustrated with photographs and prints

Troll Associates

To Tom and Tina

PICTURE CREDITS
AP/Wide World Photos, 13, 52, 81; courtesy of Harold J. Catchpole, 75; *East Anglian Daily Times,* 78; Guillardo/TIME Magazine, 17; Missouri Historical Society, W.P. Strickland, 30; National Maritime Museum, San Francisco, 59; New Zealand Embassy, 57; NOAA, 84-85; Oregon Historical Society, 63; Organization of American States, 40-41, 43, 45; *The Racing Pigeon,* 73; Royal Canadian Mounted Police, 90, 92; Clair F. Stahl, 66; UPI/Bettmann Newsphotos, 25; U.S. Navy, 50.

A TROLL BOOK, published by Troll Associates,
Mahwah, NJ 07430

Published by arrangement with The Putnam & Grosset Group. For information address The Putnam & Grosset Group, 51 Madison Avenue, New York, New York 10010.

First Troll Printing, 1988

Printed in the United States of America.

10   9   8   7   6   5   4   3   2   1

ISBN 0-8167-1371-5

CONTENTS

Introduction

Life can be strange at times. It can also be puzzling. The stories here tell of ten happenings that are both strange and puzzling. There is buried treasure that has never been found, strange disappearances, the amazing actions of animals.

Some of the mysteries described in this book are hundreds of years old. However, most of them took place in the twentieth century. All of them are true mysteries.

Information about the mysteries came from newspapers, magazines, books, and letters. Harold Catchpole wrote an eight-page letter about Mercury, the real-life pigeon in the story called "Top Secret Message." The Danish Resistance Museum sent added information about Mercury from a Danish parachutist who was in the plane with Mercury.

A few of the mysteries told about in *Strange Mysteries* have already been solved. Some may never be solved. At least one mystery will be solved in the future. In 1992, the British War Office will tell what Mercury's secret message said.

1

THE STRANGE DISAPPEARANCE OF MANUEL CORTES

Whatever happened to Manuel Cortes? It was a question often asked in Mijas. Mijas is a village in Spain. In March of 1939, Cortes disappeared. Neither police nor friends could find him. But strangely, his family didn't spend much time looking for him. Nor did they seem overly saddened by his disappearance. In fact, Cortes's family seemed to go about their daily business just as they always had.

But if Cortes's family didn't miss him, the

people of the village did. Cortes had grown up there. He was a bright youngster. And he loved school. In those days parents had to pay for their children's schooling. However, Manuel's father, a poor man, was a barber. The village schoolmaster gave Manuel a place in his school. In return, the schoolmaster was given free shaves and haircuts.

Rich and poor went to the same school. But the teacher paid almost no attention to the poor. He spent most of his time with the children of the rich. Because the teacher was friendly with his father, Manuel received his fair share of the teacher's time.

When he grew up, Manuel became a barber, too. He also joined the army for a while. The people of the village thought highly of Manuel. While still a young man, he was elected mayor. Remembering how unfair his school had been to poor children, Manuel fought for equal rights for all. He and some friends also started a union of workers.

In 1936, war broke out. The people of Spain broke up into two groups: the Republicans and the Nationalists. The Nationalists wanted Spain to be ruled by one man. The Republicans wanted the people to have a part in the government. They wanted Spain to keep on being a republic. The two groups began fighting each other. Manuel sided with the Republicans, but the Nationalists were soon winning. Manuel joined the Republican army. He spent a year helping the wounded.

The bloody war finally ended in 1939. Manuel returned home late one night. He had been on the losing side. He expected to be sent to jail for two or three years. But Juliana, his wife, told him he would most likely be shot for his beliefs. Several of his friends had already been put to death.

Manuel disappeared. He was not seen on the streets of Mijas or anywhere else.

The police came many times to Manuel's house. They questioned Juliana. They questioned his father. But the police never found Manuel. It was as though the earth had opened up and swallowed him.

The years passed. Spain was ruled by a

man by the name of Franco. Franco had been in charge of the Nationalists since 1936. Franco was a tough leader. Often, he punished those who didn't go along with him.

Then on March 28, 1969, Franco had a change of heart. He pardoned all those who had sided with the Republicans. A week later a paper telling of the pardon reached the town hall at Mijas. On the very next day, the front door of Juliana Cortes's house swung open. Out walked Manuel Cortes. People gasped when they heard the news. They hadn't seen Manuel in 30 years. It was as though he had returned from the dead.

Manuel had an amazing story to tell. When Manuel returned to his village in 1939 and learned that he might be shot, he thought about running away. Maybe he could slip into France. Or he could run off to the mountains. But there was a chance that he would be caught. And, besides, he would have to leave his family behind. Manuel decided to live in the walls of his parents' house. No one had seen him come into the

General Franco was a tough leader.

village. People would just figure he had never returned.

Juliana and Manuel's cousin chopped a

hole in the wall. A large picture was placed over the opening. During the day, Manuel lived in the wall. The space inside the wall was cramped. There wasn't even enough room for a regular chair. Manuel sat all day in a child's chair. His shoulders barely fit between the walls. At night, when no one was around, he came out. He slept in a small bed downstairs.

Later, Juliana moved to a larger home. She had been living in a small house not far from Manuel's father's home. There had been no place in her small home for Manuel to hide. In the new home, Manuel had a room of his own on the second floor. And he also had a hiding place in case the police came to search the house.

To get to the new house, Manuel dressed as an old woman. Then he sneaked into the house in the middle of a rainy winter night.

Juliana shook with fear the night they moved. But she couldn't help laughing at her husband. He looked so funny. He didn't know how to walk in the long dress. He kept tripping on it. He hopped down the street like some sort of rabbit. Luckily, no one spotted him.

Manuel watched the world through a small opening in the shutters. Or he would peek out an upstairs window. He often wished that he could call out to the people in the street below. But, of course, he couldn't.

Juliana made money for Manuel and their daughter, Maria. At first, she sold eggs. Then she sold a grass known as *esparto*. It was used to make cloth and other products. Although in hiding, Manuel tied the long stalks of *esparto* into bundles. He also kept track of how much *esparto* was sold.

When Manuel and Juliana moved to their new home, Juliana had a long talk with Maria, their daughter. "If the police find out your father is here," she said, "they will shoot him. And they will throw us in jail!" Maria knew she did not want that to happen. She hardly ever brought friends home. When she did, her father would stay hidden away until the friends left. And he would be very still so Maria's friends wouldn't hear him.

As the years passed, Manuel's daughter, Maria, grew into a young woman. She never told anyone about her father except the man she was to marry. Manuel, of course, couldn't go to Maria's wedding. He saw his daughter through the keyhole of his room.

In 1949, after ten years in hiding, Manuel nearly escaped. He planned to sneak to Barcelona, a large city in Spain. From there he would sail to France. A dock worker would get Manuel fake papers so that he could travel. But a crane fell on the dock worker. He was killed. With no way to get travel papers, Manuel gave up his plan.

There were a lot of close calls for Manuel. One day he forgot to close the door to his room. A visitor spotted him. Juliana explained that the man was her brother. Twice Manuel became very ill. Both times Juliana was able to get him the right medicine. Manuel couldn't go the dentist. When a tooth started hurting too badly, he had to pull it himself.

Manuel Cortes was 64 years old when he regained his freedom.

Over the years, Manuel never gave up hope. He was never sorry for his beliefs or that he had been on the losing side in the war. When he finally took his walk into freedom in April of 1969, he was 64 years old. He had gone into hiding at the age of 34. He had spent the best years of his life as a prisoner in his own home.

2

THE MISSING CROWN JEWELS

Sir Arthur Vicars pulled open the safe's heavy door. Everything seemed fine. The red leather case was just where it should be. So were the smaller wooden cases. Sir Arthur picked up the leather case. It was the one that held the crown jewels of Ireland. The case felt light. Or was it just his imagination? Quickly, Sir Arthur snapped open the case's lid. A neatly folded piece of tissue paper dropped to the floor. The case was empty.

"The jewels are gone!" Sir Arthur shouted. With hands shaking, Sir Arthur opened the other cases. All were empty. Sir Arthur thought he was going to pass out. He was living his worst nightmare.

In 1907, the year they disappeared, the crown jewels were worth $250,000. The pieces were made up of hundreds of sparkling diamonds and dozens of costly emeralds. Today they would be worth two or three million dollars.

Sir Arthur sent for his assistants. And then he called the police. Everyone was shocked by the crime. The jewels were kept in a safe in a locked room in a castle in Dublin, Ireland. The castle was guarded by soldiers. And the police had an office in the castle. How could a thief have gotten into the castle without being spotted?

A team of detectives examined every square inch of the castle. They also questioned Sir Arthur and his assistants. It was Sir Arthur's job to keep a history of Ireland's most important families and to watch over the jewels. They were kept in the castle to be worn by the king of England whenever he visited Ireland. Sir Arthur was known as a very careful person. But he couldn't even say when the jewels were stolen. He hadn't checked the safe for more than three weeks.

Men from the company that made the safe looked it over very carefully. There were no marks on it. This meant that the lock hadn't been picked or forced. Otherwise, there would have been tiny scratches on the metal.

The thieves must have had a key. But Sir Arthur had the only pair of keys to the safe. He kept one key with him at all times. The other was hidden in his home. Could someone have stolen one of his keys, made a copy, and then returned it without Sir Arthur knowing it was missing? It would have been difficult to do. The key was not a simple one. It would have taken a while to make a copy of it.

The more the police looked into the crime, the more puzzled they became. The robber had been very neat. Instead of grabbing all the cases and running, he had taken the jewels from their cases. After carefully unwrapping the paper in which the jewels had been placed, he had folded the empty paper and returned it to the cases.

DUBLIN METROPOLITAN POLICE.

£1,000 REWARD

STOLEN

From a Safe in the Office of Arms, Dublin Castle, during the past month, supposed by means of a false key.

GRAND MASTER'S DIAMOND STAR.

A Diamond Star of the Grand Master of the Order of St. Patrick, composed of brilliants (Brazilian stones) of the purest water, 4½ by 4½ inches, consisting of eight points, four greater and four lesser, issuing from a centre enclosing a cross of rubies and a trefoil of emeralds surrounding a sky blue enamel circle with words, "Quis Separabit, MDCCLXXXIII." In rose diamonds engraved on back. Value about £14,000.

COLLAR BADGE OF KNIGHT COMPANION.

Five collars of Knight's Companions of the Order of St. Patrick, composed of 18ct. gold, hall-marked, with roses and harps alternately tied together with knots of gold, the roses enamelled alternately, white leaves within red and red leaves within white, in the centre of the Collar an Imperial Jewelled Crown surmounting a Harp of Gold.

One of the Collars has attached a Circular Badge of the Order, composed wholly of enamel. Some of the Collars are stamped with the maker's name, "West and Son, 18 and 19 College Green, Dublin." Value £3,050.

Most of the Collars had names and dates of investiture of past Knights of the Order engraved on the backs of links.

A dark morocco leather Jewel Box, about 8 x 5 x 4½ inches, with Bramah lock and black stiff cloth cover, lined with green velvet, fitted with tray, with divisions and place for rings, containing the following:

EAR RINGS—A large and long Drop, with large oval diamond in centre, set in silver to the front and gold at back; Brazilian stones set clear, brilliant cut; a large oval Brazilian diamond Drop, brilliant cut, similarly set; a pair of Brazilian diamond Earrings, with small Drops.

BROOCH—A large pink topaz Brooch, set round with diamonds, with pink topaz pendant with diamonds.

RINGS:—A half hoop Ring of 5 large Brazilian brilliants, clear setting; an old half hoop Ring, double row of small Brazilian diamonds; a half hoop Ring of 6 pearls; a gold Ring with diamond in centre and opal at each side; a light blue enamel Ring with small conventional shaped enamel leaves, with a diamond between each leaf all round, one diamond missing; a Ring set with a ruby or almondine in centre, with white stone on each side, probably white sapphires; a very old ring having two hands in white enamel, with ruffles set with rubies at each wrist, holding a heart-shaped diamond in old fashioned silver setting, surmounted by 3 diamonds, giving the appearance of a crowned heart.

Value of contents of box, about £1,500.

GRAND MASTER'S DIAMOND BADGE.

A Diamond Badge of the Grand Master of the Order of St. Patrick, set in silver containing a trefoil in emeralds on a ruby cross surrounded by a sky blue enamelled circle with "Quis Separabit MDCCLXXXIII." In rose diamonds, surmounted by a wreath of trefoils in emeralds, the whole enclosed by a circle of large single Brazilian stones of the finest water, surmounted by a crowned harp in diamonds and loop, also in Brazilian stones. Total size of oval 3 by 2½ inches; height, 5½ inches. Value £16,000.

The above Reward will be paid to any person giving such information as will lead to the apprehension of the thief and the recovery of the property or in proportion to the amount recovered.

Police Officers are requested to cause diligent search and inquiries to be made amongst Dealers in diamonds, or other such persons, or those who may have purchased any of these articles, or received them as security, and to communicate any information obtained to

JOHN LOWE,
Superintendent.

Detective Department, Exchange Court,
Dublin, 10th July, 1907.

A reward of 1,000 pounds was offered for information leading to the return of the jewels.

One of the pieces of jewelry had a blue ribbon attached to it. The robber had taken it off and left it in the safe. The ribbon had been attached with tiny screws. The robber would have needed a very small screwdriver. It would be the type that a watchmaker might use. Taking out the screws would have taken several minutes. "Why had the robber been so careful with the ribbon?" the detectives wondered. Most crooks want to make a fast getaway.

The detectives believed the robbery was an inside job. Only an insider, they reasoned, could have gotten the key. And only someone who knew the castle well would have been able to sneak inside.

The robbery couldn't have come at a worse time. The king of England, Edward VII, was coming for a visit to Ireland. Edward VII loved fine things. He looked forward to wearing the Irish crown jewels. After talking to the police, Sir Arthur sent a telegram to Edward VII. At the time, Edward was on the royal yacht and was headed for Ireland.

After reading the telegram, Edward became very angry. "The jewels must be found!" he shouted.

Scotland Yard was brought into the case. Scotland Yard is headquarters for world-famous police officers. They work in the city of London. They didn't usually work on crimes that had taken place in Ireland. But, of course, it isn't every day that the crown jewels are stolen.

The jewels didn't have the same meaning for many of the people of Ireland as they did for Edward. At that time all of Ireland was under English rule. Large numbers of the Irish people wanted to set up their own government. They laughed and cheered when they learned that the jewels had been stolen. They thought it was a grand joke that the jewels had been slipped out of the castle right under the noses of British soldiers who were supposed to be guarding the castle.

Some people believe that the jewels were stolen by Irishmen who wanted freedom from English rule. They may have purposely

King Edward VII visited Ireland shortly after the jewels were stolen.

timed the theft to take place just before Edward's visit. It may have been their way of embarrassing the king.

Some of the detectives believed one of Sir

Arthur's assistants had taken the jewels. The assistant owed a lot of money. He may have stolen the jewels to get some quick cash. There was only one problem with this idea. The assistant was in London at the time of the robbery. To this day, it is not known who stole the jewels.

King Edward blamed Sir Arthur for the loss of the jewels. He thought Sir Arthur had been too careless. Sir Arthur and his assistants were fired or asked to quit.

Meanwhile, the hunt for the jewels went on. Homes were searched. Jewelers all over the world were questioned. Even dreams were checked. One woman reported dreaming that the jewels were buried on a farm. The farm was dug up. But no jewels were found.

In September of 1931, someone got in touch with the police in Dublin. By that time, Ireland had been divided. The southern part was now free and became known as the Republic of Ireland. Dublin was located in the Republic of Ireland. The person calling the police was willing to turn the jewels in. But the person wanted to make a deal. The police did not believe the caller. No deal was made. And the jewels were not returned.

The years passed. It looked as though the jewels were gone forever. Then in 1983, an old woman in Ireland had a strange story to tell the police. Some fifty years before, in the early 1930s, the woman's grandmother had shown her where the jewels were buried. The grandmother told the granddaughter that the hiding place was to be kept a secret. However, the young woman could let the secret be known in 50 years.

The woman kept her silence for all those years. Hearing her secret, the police searched the place that she pointed out. Bulldozers were used. So were tools that can find hidden metal. But they did no good. The police found nothing. If anything, the missing crown jewels of Ireland were more of a mystery than ever.

3

THE CODE NO ONE CAN BREAK

Do the numbers 71, 194, 38, 1701, 89, and 76 mean anything to you? If they do, you might have the key to becoming very rich. These numbers are part of a code that tells the whereabouts of a buried treasure.

In April, 1817, Thomas Jefferson Beale headed west. With him were 29 other men. They planned to hunt buffalo and bears. They ended up becoming a part of one of the most puzzling mysteries of all time.

After a hard day of chasing after a herd of buffalo, a group of Beale's men set up camp.

A sparkle of metal caught the eye of one of the hunters. With his knife, the hunter dug out a sliver of yellowish metal from a large rock. "Gold!" he cried. "I've found gold!" The hunters found that many of the rocks were speckled with gold and silver. Beale called off the hunt and began mining instead.

The gold and silver cast a spell on the men. For the next five years, they spent nearly every waking hour digging metal from the earth.

Beale and some of the other men made two trips back to his home in the East. Each time his wagons were loaded with iron cooking pots crammed with gold and silver. On his second trip, he stopped off in St. Louis, Missouri. Beale wanted to see Monsieur Pierre, a friend. He traded Pierre some of the gold for jewels. The jewels took up less room and so there would be fewer pots to carry.

Beale and his men carefully hid the treasure. The heavy pots were buried six feet underground and covered with large stones and dirt.

Many hunters went west in the 1800s, just as Beale and his men had done.

Later, the men grew worried. What if they were all killed? All that treasure would just stay buried. Their families wouldn't even know about it.

The men decided that Beale should tell someone else about the treasure. Beale chose Robert Morriss. Morriss was the owner of a hotel. He seemed to be a hard-working, honest person. Just to be on the safe side, Beale made up a code. In his code, Beale used numbers instead of letters to write words. Beale then wrote three separate papers. All were in code. One described the treasure. A second told where it was hidden. And the third listed the people who should share the treasure if anything happened to Beale and the other men. Then Beale wrote two letters to Morriss in regular English.

Beale gave Morriss an iron box. Locked in the box were the two letters and the three coded papers. Beale asked Morriss if he would hold the box for him. Morriss agreed. Beale told Morriss to open the box if he didn't return within ten years. Beale, however, didn't tell what the papers in the box were.

As he headed back to the mine, Beale wondered if he had told Morriss enough. Stopping off in St. Louis, he sent Morriss a long letter. The letter was dated May 9, 1822. The letter explained that the contents of the box were valuable to many people. It said that some of the papers in the box were in code. The key to the code would be sent to Morriss in ten years.

As he promised, Beale put the key to the code in an envelope. He then gave the envelope to his friend in St. Louis. The envelope was addressed to Morriss. Also written on the envelope was the message, "Not to be delivered until June, 1832."

Shortly after writing to Morriss, Beale and ten of his men were on their way to the mine. It was to be their last trip. They were never heard from again. The men back at the mine also vanished.

June of 1832 came and went. But the key to the code was not delivered. And Morriss didn't break open the iron box. Morriss didn't open the box until 1845.

The two letters in the box told of the buried treasure. The letters explained that the coded papers would tell exactly where the treasure was buried. One letter also promised Morriss a share of the treasure. Without the key, Morriss was not able to make any sense out of the coded papers. Over the years, in spare moments, Morriss tried to figure out the code. But he got nowhere. Finally, in 1862 he showed the papers to a friend, James P. Ward.

For Ward, the papers became a curse. Before long, Ward was spending all his time and money in efforts to break the code. After years of trying, he finally broke the code for one of the pages.

The key to the code was the Declaration of Independence. Ward numbered the words in the Declaration of Independence. Then he matched up the numbers on the page in code with the first letters of the words in the Declaration of Independence. The letters

The key to one of the coded pages was the Declaration of Independence.

formed an amazing message. It told that Beale had buried hundreds of pounds of gold, silver, and jewels. However, it didn't tell exactly where the treasure was buried. That was described in one of the other papers.

With shaking hands, Ward used the key with the other pages. It didn't work. Beale, it seems, had used a different key for each page.

Crazed by being so close to the secret, Ward spent nearly every waking moment trying to break the code. He stayed at it for 20 long years. During that time, he lost his friends and his health. He ruined his family's happiness and spent all his money. Still, he kept on working on this code.

Finally, Ward realized there was only one way to break this evil spell. He wrote a small booklet about the treasure and coded messages. After reading the booklet, others would start trying to break the code. Then maybe Ward could put it out of his mind. He might also make some money from the sale of the booklets. Each booklet was to be sold for 50 cents.

71, 194, 38, 1701, 89, 76, 11, 83, 1629, 48, 94,
63, 132, 16, 111, 95, 84, 341, 975, 14, 40, 64, 27,
81, 139, 213, 63, 90, 1120, 8, 15, 3, 126, 2018, 40,
74, 758, 485, 604, 230, 436, 664, 582, 150, 251, 284,
308, 231, 124, 211, 486, 225, 401, 370, 11, 101, 305,
139, 189, 17, 33, 88, 208, 193, 145, 1, 94, 73, 416,
918, 263, 28, 500, 538, 356, 117, 136, 219, 27, 176,
130, 10, 460, 25, 485, 18, 436, 65, 84, 200, 283,
118, 320, 138, 36, 416, 280 15, 71, 224, 961, 44, 16,
401, 39, 88, 61, 304, 12, 21, 24, 283, 134, 92, 63,
246, 486, 682, 7, 219, 184, 360, 780, 18, 64, 463,
474, 131, 160, 79, 73, 440, 95, 18, 64, 581, 34, 69,
128, 367, 460, 17, 81, 12, 103, 820, 62, 116, 97, 103,
862, 70, 60, 1317, 471, 540, 208, 121, 890, 346, 36,
150, 59, 568, 614, 13, 120, 63, 219, 812, 2160, 1780,
99, 35, 18, 21, 136, 872, 15, 28, 170, 88, 4, 30, 44,
112, 18, 147, 436, 195, 320, 37, 122, 113, 6, 140,
8, 120, 305, 42, 58, 461, 44, 106, 301, 13, 408, 680,
93, 86, 116, 530, 82, 568, 9, 102, 38, 416, 89, 71,
216, 728, 965, 818, 2, 38, 121, 195, 14, 326, 148,
234, 18, 55, 131, 234, 361, 824, 5, 81, 623, 48, 961,
19, 26, 33, 10, 1101, 365, 92, 88, 181, 275, 346, 201,
206, 86, 36, 219, 320, 829, 840, 68, 326, 19, 48, 122,
85, 216, 284, 919, 861, 326, 985, 233, 64, 68, 232,
431, 960, 50, 29, 81, 216, 321, 603, 14, 612, 81, 360,
36, 51, 62, 194, 78, 60, 200, 314, 676, 112, 4, 28,
18, 61, 136, 247, 819, 921, 1060, 464, 895, 10, 6,
66, 119, 38, 41, 49, 602, 423, 962, 302, 294, 875,
78, 14, 23, 111, 109, 62, 31, 501, 823, 216, 280, 34,
24, 150, 1000, 162, 286, 19, 21, 17, 340, 19, 242,
31, 86, 234, 140, 607, 115, 33, 191, 67, 104, 86, 52,
88, 16, 80, 121, 67, 95, 122, 216, 548, 96, 11, 201,
77, 364, 218, 65, 667, 890, 236, 154, 211, 10, 98,
34, 119, 56, 216, 119, 71, 218, 1164, 1496, 1817, 51,
39, 210, 36, 3, 19, 540, 232, 22, 141, 617, 84, 290,
80, 46, 207, 411, 150, 29, 38, 46, 172, 85, 194, 36,
261, 543, 897, 624, 18, 212, 416, 127, 931, 19, 4, 63,
96, 12, 101, 418, 16, 140, 230, 460, 538, 19, 27,
88, 612, 1431, 90, 716, 275, 74, 83, 11, 426, 89,
72, 84, 1300, 1706, 814, 221, 132, 40, 102, 34, 858,
975, 1101, 84, 16, 79, 23, 16, 81, 122, 324, 403, 912,
227, 936, 447, 55, 86, 34, 43, 212, 107, 96, 314, 264,
1065, 323, 428 601, 203, 124, 95, 216, 814, 2906,
654, 820, 2, 301, 112, 176, 213, 71, 87, 96, 202, 35,
10, 2, 41, 17, 84, 221, 736, 820, 214, 11, 60, 760.

As it turned out, most of the booklets were destroyed in a fire. Only a few people got to read the booklet.

One of those who got a copy of the booklet was Clayton Hart. Hart spent nearly 40 years trying to break the code. But he failed. Scientists, code experts, and computer experts have also tried to figure out Beale's messages. They didn't do any better than Ward did.

Some people wonder whether there really is a buried treasure. Maybe it was all a trick or some kind of sick joke. Others wonder about Beale. Searchers have not been able to prove that anyone by that name ever lived.

Some people believe that there really was a Beale and that he buried the treasure. But they believe the treasure has been dug up. The pots at the end of the coded rainbow could be empty.

Left: This coded paper tells where the treasure is hidden.

4

THE BURIED TREASURE OF COCOS ISLAND

John Keating met Thompson soon after boarding the ship bound from England to Canada. There was something about Thompson that interested Keating. Thompson seemed to know some deep, dangerous secret. During the trip, the two become good friends.

Keating invited Thompson to live in his home in Newfoundland. Later, deathly ill, Thompson asked Keating to come close. Thompson had a secret to share. Years ago, in 1820, Lima, a city in Peru, had been under attack. The Spanish, who ruled Peru then, gathered about $20 million in gold, silver, and jewels. Thompson had been a sea captain. The Spanish asked Thompson to take the treasure to another port for safekeeping.

Thompson agreed. But he had a change of heart when he thought about the riches aboard his ship. He and his men killed the Spanish soldiers who were guarding the treasure. Thompson set sail for Cocos Island. Cocos is a small jungle island in the Pacific Ocean. It isn't far from Costa Rica. Pirates had been using it for years to hide their stolen treasures.

Thompson and his men used rowboats to carry the treasure from the ship to the island. They buried eleven boatloads of treasure. Later, Thompson's ship was captured by a Spanish warship. All but two of the men were put to death. Thompson and another man escaped. However, a tiger shark put an end to the other man. Thompson was then the only person alive who knew where the treasure was hidden.

After telling the tale to Keating, Thompson, gasping for breath, pointed to a corner of the room. "In my sea chest," he whispered, "you'll find a long paper of writing which will tell you how to find the treasure." Moments later, Thompson passed away.

Keating studied the paper carefully. On the paper was a map of Cocos Island. Directions were printed beneath the map:

Much of Cocos Island is covered with . . .

"Once there, follow the coastline of the bay till you find a creek . . . At high-water mark, you go up the bed of a stream which flows inland. Now you step out seventy paces, west by south . . . Against the skyline you will see the gap in the hills. From any other place, the gap is invisible. Turn north and walk to a stream. You will now see a

. . . thick bushes and tall trees.

rock with a smooth face ... At the height of a man's shoulder above the ground, you will see a hole large enough for you to insert your thumb. Thrust in an iron bar, twist it ... And you will find a door which opens on the treasure!"

Thoughts of treasure filled Keating's mind. He teamed up with a man by the name of Captain Bogue. Keating had the map. Bogue had the ship. Keating and Bogue had no trouble finding the treasure. It was just where the map said it would be.

Loaded with treasure, the two headed back to the ship. A heavy wave tipped over their small boat. Dragged down by the gold hidden in secret pockets, Bogue sank to the bottom. Keating's pockets were heavy with treasure, too. But he clung to the side of the overturned boat as it drifted out to sea. Picked up by a passing ship, Keating returned to Newfoundland.

Arriving home, he spread out a treasure of gold coins and jewels for his wife to see. The treasure was worth about $100,000.

One hunter chipped his name in this rock in 1846.

Still, thousands of pounds of gold, silver, and jewels had been left behind on the island. Before leaving, Bogue and Keating had sealed up the hiding place.

After Keating's death, his wife sailed to Cocos Island to search for the treasure. But she returned empty-handed. By this time, the secret of the treasure was a secret no more. Keating had told his wife, a friend, and a servant about the treasure. The servant let several of his friends know about the secret. Word of the treasure spread quickly. Treasure hunters from around the world headed for Cocos Island to try their luck. Some stayed only a few days. But one man remained for 17 years.

August Gissler set up a home on Cocos Island in 1891. In time, Costa Rica, which owns Cocos Island, made Gissler governor of the island. Costa Rica also said that Gissler was the only person allowed to hunt for the treasure. In return, Gissler promised to give Costa Rica half of what he found.

Not much attention was paid to Gissler's rights. In fact, the trickle of treasure hunters became a flood. Once a British warship stopped by. Some 300 sailors hacked away at the thick jungle but found nothing.

In his 17 years on Cocos Island, Gissler found only 33 gold coins. That comes out to about two gold coins for each year spent

The treasure hunter has a drink of coconut milk.

on Cocos. Finally, Gissler gave up and moved to New York City.

Over the years, Cocos Island has not stayed the same. Landslides have changed the look of the island. They may even have covered the spot where the treasure was buried. Trees, vines, and bushes have also grown taller and thicker. Treasure maps from long ago may no longer be useful.

There are a number of treasure maps for Cocos Islands. Which ones are fake? Which ones are real? No one can say. Maybe they're all fakes. Even if the maps are real, the treasure may have been hauled away years ago.

There is a mysterious wooden marker that was found on Cocos Island. The marker says, "The bird has flown." Some people believe this message means the treasure is gone.

Even if the treasure is still on Cocos Island, no one may hunt for it. Costa Rica made Cocos Island a park in 1978. Treasure hunting is no longer allowed there.

5

THE MYSTERY OF THE MISSING DIVERS

There seemed to be a curse on the Spanish ship. One stormy night, about 300 years ago, she smashed into a jagged rock near Malpelo Island. Malpelo Island is not too far from Buena Ventura, Colombia. The rock tore open the wooden hull. The ship soon sank. All hands were lost, except one. Clinging to a floating timber, the sailor rode the waves to a deserted island.

Weeks passed by before he was picked up from the island. By that time, he was barely alive. He had to be carried off the island. He died a few days later. But before he died, he described the ship's rich cargo. The ship had been loaded with gold and silver.

Over the years many tries had been made to bring up the ship's gold and silver. But they all ended the same way. The crew on the salvage ship would feel sharp tugs on the lifeline. The lifeline is a strong rope tied to the ship's deck and then attached to the diver. The crew would start hauling the diver up. Then suddenly the lifeline would become limp. When the lifeline and the air hose reached the surface, there would be no one attached to them. Both had been snapped apart. The diver was at the bottom of the ocean. With his air supply cut off, he was dead.

This happened not once or twice but seven times. The sunken schooner got a bad name. Divers refused to work anywhere near it. They didn't care how much gold and silver was stored in its holds. To the divers, the ship and its treasure seemed cursed.

Harry Rieseberg didn't believe in curses. When Boyer, a friend, asked Rieseberg to dive for the ship's treasure, Rieseberg agreed.

Still, Rieseberg was extra careful when he made his first dive. In case he had forgotten about the divers, there was something to remind him inside the wreck. Rieseberg tripped over a diver's copper helmet lying in the ship's doorway. A pale skeleton grinned up at him. Then something bubbled across his helmet. It was the air from his hose. His hose had been snapped apart. Air was leaking from his suit.

Rieseberg was in serious trouble. The pressure deep beneath the sea is very strong. The air pressure in the suit kept the pressure of the sea from crushing him. But if all the air leaked out of the suit, the sea's pressure would squeeze the life out of Rieseberg.

Quickly Rieseberg shut off the air valve that let air flow into his suit. Otherwise, with the hose cut, the air would rush out of the suit. With the valve shut, the air in his suit would last about five more minutes. Rieseberg gave his lifeline a hard yank.

Divers who come up too fast get the "bends." This can make a diver seriously ill or even kill him. When he was about halfway

up, Rieseberg rested for a moment. This gave his body a little time to get used to the change in air pressure. The rest was long enough to save Rieseberg's life. But he felt stiff and sore when he was pulled aboard the ship.

After taking it easy for a few days, Rieseberg was ready to try another dive. He figured a sharp rock or broken timber had sliced his air hose. This time he would watch more closely.

Rieseberg reached the ship's hold with no problem. He soon found the treasure. He was about to return to the surface when a large piece of cloth caught his eye. Picking up the cloth, he discovered a metal statue. The statue's eyes were two jewels. Nearby were two skeletons. Shaking with horror, Rieseberg headed for the doorway. He didn't make it.

Crowded into the doorway was a giant octopus. The mystery of the missing divers

Left: Rieseberg put on a diving suit much like the one worn by this Navy diver.

Rieseberg spotted a giant octopus.

was solved! The octopus had killed them.
And now it was after Rieseberg.

As the octopus oozed toward him, Rieseberg slipped his shark knife out of its holder.
Then he backed into a corner. A slimy arm
whipped across the room. Rieseberg sliced

52

it off. Two more tentacles immediately wound around his body. Rieseberg hacked himself free.

The beast squirted a cloud of thick ink at the diver. A fourth tentacle swished through the water. Rieseberg chopped at it blindly. The tentacle plopped onto a pile of sand.

Rieseberg seemed to be winning. Then another tentacle crashed into his helmet and drove him into the wall. Rieseberg crumbled into a heap but soon pulled himself to his feet. Once again, he slashed free of the octopus. But the creature hooked onto his left arm.

Trying to get loose, Rieseberg dropped his knife. Tightening its grip, the octopus started pulling Rieseberg to its deadly beak. Looking about wildly, Rieseberg spotted the knife. He grabbed it with his right hand and jammed it into the creature's ugly body.

The octopus ripped an opening in Rieseberg's suit. The diver dropped to the deck as air bubbles whooshed out of his suit. A black curtain was falling over his eyes.

Slowly the curtain lifted. Rieseberg was looking up at Boyer, the friend who had planned the treasure hunt. "What happened?" Rieseberg mumbled weakly.

Boyer filled him in. The crew knew nothing of Rieseberg's fight with the octopus. His lifeline had become tangled so they couldn't feel any tugs. As time passed, Boyer became worried. Two divers were sent down. They found Rieseberg lying on the sand. Three octopus arms were wrapped around his body. But the octopus was dead.

Luckily, there was still air in the suit. The divers shut off the valve to keep air from escaping. They then carried Rieseberg to the surface. It had been a close call.

6

WHATEVER HAPPENED TO JACK?

It's known as French Pass, but maybe it should be called Shipwreck Pass. The passage from Pelorus Sound to Tasman Bay off the coast of New Zealand is one of the most dangerous waterways in the world. Swirling waters and jagged rocks hidden just beneath the surface have sunk dozens of ships.

For the crew of the *Brindle*, the short trip through the pass seemed to take forever. The *Brindle* was a sailing ship from Boston that was headed for Sydney, Australia. A heavy rain beat down upon the ship. High waves rocked against her sides. One of the lookouts spotted a fin in the water. Was it a shark? A whale? Peering through the thick sheets of rain, it was hard to tell what it was. Spotting a large tail, one of the crew reached for a harpoon. Whales were worth a lot of money in the 1870s. Seeing the harpoon, the captain's wife called to the sailor. She ordered the man to put the harpoon down.

The creature turned out to be a dolphin. A speedy animal, the dolphin could easily have raced away. But it didn't. In fact, it was acting very strangely. It kept on leaping out of the water in front of the ship. When the ship fell behind, the dolphin waited for it. It seemed to be leading the ship. By following the dolphin, the *Brindle* sailed safely through the pass with no trouble at all.

Once the ship was through the pass, the dolphin swam back toward Pelorus Sound. The crew waved good-bye and thanked the dolphin for his help.

Soon the dolphin was leading other ships through the pass. To both crew and passen-

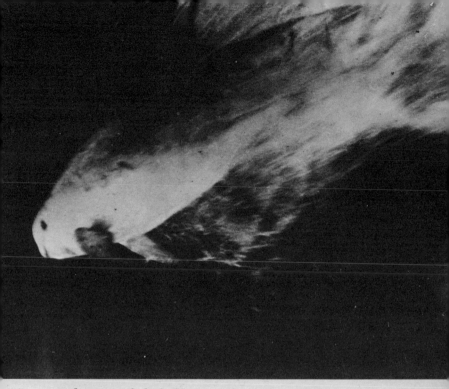

Pelorus Jack led ships safely through the sound.

gers, he was a welcome sight. Somehow, the dolphin seemed to know just where the dangerous parts of the pass were. He guided ships around them.

In time, crews sailing through the pass named the helpful dolphin. He usually met the ships in Pelorus Sound. He came to be known as Pelorus Jack.

In 1903, a sailor aboard a ship called the *Penguin* had too much to drink. He picked up a rifle and shot at Pelorus Jack. Pelorus Jack disappeared. The sailor was locked up.

Hearing of the sailor's drunken action, lawmakers in New Zealand passed a law. Anyone harming Pelorus Jack would be fined 100 pounds. In those days, that would have been close to $500.

The days passed. No sign was seen of Pelorus Jack. People feared the worst. They believed the dolphin was dead. Then suddenly, two weeks later, Pelorus Jack was back. The sailor's cruel action could have turned Jack against people. But it didn't. He kept on guiding ships through the pass. All ships, that is, except one. He never went near the *Penguin* again. The *Penguin* came to be known as a bad-luck ship. Later, she smashed into some rocks and sank.

Pelorus Jack became famous. Songs were sung about him. A movie showed how he guided ships. Even a candy bar was named after the good-hearted guide. People began

Pelorus Jack guided ships like this one.

making trips through the pass just to see Pelorus Jack. When he leaped out of the water, they would shout excitedly.

Then Pelorus Jack was seen no more. It was 1912. Pelorus Jack had been guiding ships from Pelorus Sound to Tasman Bay for some 40 years. Now he had disappeared. Had he grown old and died? Had he been shot or harpooned? Was he tired of guiding ships? No one could say. Nor could they say why he had helped ships all those years. And they couldn't figure out how he knew that the ships needed to be guided.

People were saddened by Pelorus Jack's disappearance. They had a deep sense of loss. The trip through the pass would never be the same. A statue was put up to honor Pelorus Jack. It stands today on Wellington Beach in New Zealand. The statue was a way for people to say thanks to the mysterious creature who had helped keep them safe.

7

CAN A METEORITE
BE MISSING?

Dr. John Evans didn't know it, but he was about to make an amazing discovery. It was a hot day in July of 1856. John Evans was studying rocks and plants in the mountains and forests of Oregon.

Helping Evans were two fur trappers from Canada. They were big tough men. You had to be big and tough to travel through the wilds of Oregon.

The nearest town was Port Orford. And that was about 40 miles away. The three men had climbed steep mountain trails. They had cut their way through thick forests.

The trip had been so difficult that their mules had died. But Evans pushed on. He had a job to do.

From time to time, he would bend down and pick up a rock or plant. He would drop these in one of his bags. When there was too much to carry, the trappers begged him to throw away some of the rocks. But Evans threw away food instead. Later, they would run out of food. And they would be forced to eat their dogs.

For most scientists, there would also have been the danger of attack by Indians. But not for John Evans. Evans was a doctor and had taken care of many sick Indians. To the Indians, John Evans was a great man.

One day Dr. Evans was hiking up a mountain, which he called Bald Mountain. The top of the mountain was rocky and brown, but the slope was green with grass. A giant rock caught his eye. It was sticking out of the side of the mountain like a huge nose. There was something strange about the rock. First of all, it was the only large rock around.

The Willamette Meteorite was found not far from the area where Evans found his meteorite.

And, second of all, it was different from all the other rocks that Evans had collected. Evans chipped off a few pieces of the rock and put them in his bag.

After the trip was over, Evans sent a

sample of the huge rock to a science lab in Boston. Charles T. Jackson examined the sample. He was surprised by what he found. The rock sample seemed to be from a meteorite. Meteorites come from outer space.

A cautious scientist, Jackson sent a piece of the sample to Dr. W. K. Haidinger in Vienna. Vienna is a city in Europe. Haidinger had spent much of his life studying meteorites.

Haidinger's report proved that Jackson was right. The strange piece of rock was part of a meteorite. It had come from a stony-iron meteorite. It was similar to one that had been discovered in Russia 100 years before. But it was much larger. A very large meteorite must have come apart as it was falling to earth. One part had crashed into Russia. A second part had landed on the side of a mountain in Oregon.

Jackson immediately wrote to Evans with the news. Jackson wanted to know how large the meteorite was. He also wanted to know exactly where it had been found.

The rock was five feet high. And that's not counting the part buried in the ground. The rock was about three or four feet wide. It was estimated that it weighed about eleven tons. That would make it the largest stony-iron meteorite in the world.

Evans and Jackson made plans to find the meteorite and study it. Congress agreed to pay for the trip. However, Evans was struck down by a serious sickness and died. Shortly after that, the Civil War broke out. Jackson put off his travel plans. After the war ended, Congress decided it couldn't spare the money for the trip.

Before he died, Evans wrote a letter telling where he had found the meteorite. "There cannot be the least difficulty in finding the meteorite," Evans said. However, this did not prove to be true. Dozens of searchers have hunted for the meteorite. But no one has found it. There is even a club of hikers who look for the meteorite each year. But they have had no luck. For one thing, Evans' directions weren't as clear as he thought

Many mountains in Oregon are rocky and look alike. Which one was Bald Mountain?

they were. He said that the meteorite was on Bald Mountain. But as far as anyone can tell, there was no mountain with that name.

There are several mountains not far from Port Orford that have bare tops. But who can say which one is the Bald Mountain that Evans climbed?

Then, too, the land has changed over the years. Landslides may have covered the meteorite. Tall trees have sprouted up where there was just grass. The meteorite may even have rolled down the mountain and landed in a deep stream.

A few scientists say that there never was any such meteorite. Most, however, believe that Evans really did find a meteorite. They fear, though, that the world's largest stony-iron meteorite may never be found again.

8

TOP SECRET MESSAGE

In the early 1940s, England was fighting for its life. England was at war with Germany. Germany was led by a madman by the name of Adolph Hitler. Hitler wanted to rule Europe.

Hitler had a powerful army. His soldiers had already taken Poland, Norway, Denmark, France, and several other countries. Now his planes were pounding away at England. Each night bombs from German planes rained down upon England.

England was fighting back as hard as it could. It was also getting help from the underground. Many people in the countries taken by Hitler wanted to break free of his rule. They joined the underground. The underground stole German guns and blew up German trains. They also sneaked secret information about the German army to England.

In the summer of 1942, something very important was happening in northern Denmark. The English War Office needed information about the happening from the Danish underground. Two radios had been parachuted into Denmark for use by the underground. The Germans learned about the first radio. The second radio was carried by Carl Bruhn. He jumped from an English plane. Bruhn's parachute failed to open. He was killed and the radio was smashed.

There was one other way to get information from the underground. The War Office would use pigeons.

Men from the War Office were sent to 50 owners of racing pigeons. Each owner was asked to give up two pigeons. The War Office asked for 100 pigeons because the information was needed so badly. The War Office hoped that at least one of the pigeons would make it back with a message.

On the night of July 26, 1942, the pigeons were placed aboard an English plane. There was a good chance the plane would never make it. German fighter planes and gun crews on the ground had already shot down hundreds of English planes.

Luckily, the plane flew to Denmark safely. H. F. Hansen, a Danish parachutist, was aboard the plane. He remembers that the plane circled over Farsø in northern Denmark. But there was no one there to pick up the pigeons. Maybe there had been some kind of mix-up. Or maybe German soldiers had picked up the underground members who were supposed to be there. The pilot didn't know what had gone wrong. He turned around and headed for home.

On the way back, the pigeons were dropped anyway. The pigeons had been placed in small boxes that had parachutes. In the boxes were candy and cigarettes for the finder. There was also a message. It asked the finder to send any information he or she might have about the German army. The message was to be placed in a tube that had been strapped on a leg of each pigeon. It was hoped that members of the underground would find the pigeons and send the information needed by the War Office.

How many pigeons were found and given messages? That will never be known. But within a day or so, perhaps a dozen pigeons or more were sent on their way.

Each bird headed for its loft. That's what they had been trained to do. Most of the trip was over the North Sea. The North Sea stretched for several hundred miles. The birds were used to flying long distances. But their flights were usually over land. On flights over land, they could rest for a while on a rooftop or telephone line. But over the sea, there was no place to stop. Many of the pigeons flew until they could fly no more. And then they dropped to their deaths.

Sometimes a bird would fly too close to the sea. Then a giant wave would leap up without warning and snatch it out of the air.

But if flying over the sea was very dangerous, flying over land was even more so. The Germans knew that pigeons were being used to carry secret messages. There was an order to shoot all pigeons on sight. Some of the German army's best shooters lay in wait for a pigeon to fly overhead.

The hours passed. The War Office kept on checking the lofts. It was the same at loft after loft. No pigeons had returned from Denmark. Then on July 30, there was an excited call from a loft in Ipswich in Suffolk, England. Mercury, a five-year-old blue hen, had just flown in. The message was taken from the pigeon and rushed to the War Office. Because the message was secret, even the pigeon's owners were not allowed to read it.

The pigeon belonged to Jim Catchpole and his son, Harold. They were pleased to see

Mercury carried a secret message 480 miles.

their pigeon return safely. They usually had about 150 pigeons. Harold had joined the National Pigeon Service in 1939. Their pigeons had been used for several years to carry messages for the War Office. Dozens had been lost. Of the 16,554 pigeons used by the War Office from owners throughout the country, only 1,842 ever returned. Nine out of ten pigeons didn't make it.

Harold was curious. He couldn't help wondering where Mercury had been. And he wondered, too, what message she had carried. But wartime is a time of secrets. The Catchpoles were not told where their pigeons had been. And they were not told what was in the messages the pigeons carried.

It wasn't until four years later that the Catchpoles learned that Mercury had done anything special. In 1946, Mercury was awarded the Dickin Medal. That's the highest medal an animal can receive. It is given for an outstanding act of bravery. Only 53 animals have ever been given the award. Mercury was also given the Army Pigeon Service Award.

The papers that went with the awards told something of Mercury's amazing deed. The message she carried was top secret and very important. Of the many birds that had been parachuted, only Mercury had made it safely

Jim Catchpole holds cup won by one of his pigeons.

to her loft. Amazingly, she had flown 480 miles, most of it over the North Sea. Of all the pigeons that had served in the Special Section, she was said to be the most outstanding.

As the awards were being given, Harold and his dad beamed with pride. Harold thought back to 1936. That was the year Mercury had been born. Harold was a teenager then. And he had helped train Mercury. When Mercury was three months old, Harold would get up early in the morning. Then he put Mercury and other young pigeons in a basket and pedaled his bike a few miles out of town. There he would "throw" Mercury and the other pigeons one by one. Throwing is a special way of tossing a homing pigeon into the air. The pigeons would wing their way back to the loft. Harry would pedal back home for a quick breakfast. Then it was off to school.

As Mercury and the other young pigeons grew strong, Harry pedaled longer distances. Sometimes he would travel 15 miles from home. Later, the pigeons were taken by train to more distant places and then let go. When fully trained, Mercury was entered into races.

After getting her medals, Mercury became the "pride and joy" of the Catchpoles' loft. Mercury died in 1949 and was buried near the loft.

Mercury's medals were sold in 1983 for 5,000 pounds ($7,500). The medals were given to the Royal Pigeon Racing Association by a wealthy ice cream maker. The medals were put in a place of honor in a traveling museum. The traveling museum raises money for the sick. As Harry Catchpole explained, it was better that the medals help raise money for sick people than gather dust in his library.

As visitors to the museum learn about Mercury, they can't help wondering about the secret message she carried. Was it plans for some sort of surprise attack? Was it information about a new kind of gun? Did it tell about a large store of German guns or bombs?

The message that Mercury carried was top secret. The War Office doesn't tell top secrets

Harold Catchpole was pleased that Mercury's medals sold for a high price.

for 50 years. So the secret won't be told until July of 1992. On the day the secret message is shown, Harold Catchpole says he will be first in line to see it.

9

THE DESERTED LIGHTHOUSE

Joseph Moore was late for work. It was December 26. He should have been there on December 20.

Being late wasn't his fault. Moore was a keeper in a lighthouse. The lighthouse had been built on a rocky island called Eilean Mor. The island is in the Atlantic Ocean off the west coast of Scotland. The only way to get to the tiny island was by boat. For the past week it had been much too stormy for the *Hesperus* to make the trip. Any boat trying to dock at the lighthouse's landing would have been smashed on the rocks.

The lighthouse was a large one and had a crew of four. The men took turns working. They would work three weeks straight and then have two weeks off. This meant that there were always three men at the lighthouse and one back home.

Moore hoped that the man he was to work for wouldn't be too angry. Because Moore hadn't been able to get there, the man had been forced to spend Christmas at the lighthouse.

Working at the lighthouse could be boring. Day after day, you looked at the same faces. And, of course, there wasn't any place to go. The lighthouse didn't even have a boat of its own.

The men always enjoyed getting news from home. Moore was surprised that the men didn't flash a signal as the *Hesperus* drew closer. The captain of the *Hesperus* gave a blast of the boat's whistle. Still, there was no answer. "Could it be the men were still sleeping?" Moore wondered. That hardly seemed possible.

The lighthouse stood on a rocky island.

A chill wind whipped across the icy water as Moore was rowed to the lighthouse's landing in one of the *Hesperus's* small boats. Hurrying ashore, Moore began the long climb up the steps to the lighthouse. The steps, which had been cut into the steep side of the rocky island, were icy. Moore clung to the rail as he slowly made his way to the lighthouse door some 200 feet above the landing.

Moore half-expected someone to fling open the door and greet him. But there was a stillness about the lighthouse that had begun to worry him.

Tugging open the heavy wooden door of the lighthouse, Moore shouted, "Hello! Anyone about?" But there was no answer.

A wave of fear swept over Moore. He rushed up the winding stairs. He threw open the door to the lighthouse's main room. Moore hoped to see the men sitting around the table sipping tea. But the room was empty.

Glancing quickly around the room, Moore noticed that the clock was not running. It hadn't been wound. It was a cold day, but the stove was out. "This is all very strange," Moore thought to himself.

Moore ran down to the landing and called to the crew of the rowboat. "There is no one here!" he shouted. "The lighthouse is empty!"

The men could hardly believe their ears. How could that be? There was no place for the keepers to go. They had to be in the lighthouse.

Two of the crew helped Moore search the lighthouse from top to bottom. They looked in every room. They searched the outside of the lighthouse. There was no sign of the men. What could have happened to the keepers? The men hunted for clues.

The first place they looked was in the log. The log was a written record of the main things that happened each day. The last written page was dated December 15, nine o'clock in the morning. There was no note in the log telling of any trouble. Nothing was written about where the keepers had gone.

Looking in the light tower, the searchers

At times, it was too stormy for ships . . .

discovered that the morning's jobs had not been finished. The keepers had a list of things to do each day. In the morning one keeper always put out the light and cleaned the lens. Then he covered the light with a large cloth. The other jobs had been done. But the

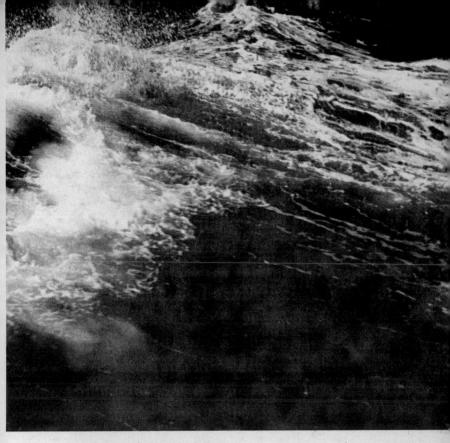

. . . to sail to the lighthouse.

light had not been covered. Why hadn't the keeper finished the job? Had he rushed off somewhere in the middle of his work? If so, where had he gone and why?

There was something else that was strange. The boots and coats belonging to two of the men were missing. The men only wore these when they went to one of the landings.

On the west side of the lighthouse, a heavy iron railing leading to the landing had been twisted. And a huge block of cement had been tossed aside. It looked as though a fierce storm had belted the lighthouse. Still, the lighthouse was not damaged inside. And the men were used to storms. They had better sense than to go outside when wind and waves were pounding the lighthouse. Besides, although there had been a storm on December 12 and 13, the log said the weather became calm on the 14th. It seems the damage was probably done on December 12 or 13.

Later, a strange discovery was made. Incoming tides sometimes created huge waves. On a perfectly calm, clear day, a giant wave would suddenly leap out of the water. It was powerful enough to snatch up anyone in its path. Could the men have been swept off the steps to the landing by an unexpected wave? It seems possible. But why would all three of them have gone out to the steps. And why did one man rush off in the middle of his work? Did he dash outside when he heard the cries of the other two men? Only three men know the answers to these questions. And they haven't been seen since December of 1900.

10

THE VILLAGE THAT DISAPPEARED

There is a story told about an Eskimo village that disappeared. According to the tale, Joe Labelle was on his way to visit some friends in the village of Anjikini in northern Canada. It was a bitterly cold day in November of 1930. Although dressed warmly, Joe shivered as he neared the village. It wasn't just the cold. He sensed that something was very wrong.

The village was off by itself. The people of Anjikini saw few outsiders. Usually they became very excited when a visitor arrived. Joe had just about reached the village. But no one had come to meet him.

Joe called out a greeting. But there was no answer. The village was deathly quiet. Joe ran from hut to hut. Each was empty. There were signs, though, that the people had left in a hurry. In some of the huts, pots of food were found. The food was burned. The cooking fires were piles of ashes. It was as though someone had run out in the middle of cooking dinner.

A sealskin jacket lay on the floor of a large hut. A sewing needle was sticking out of the partly sewn jacket. Something or someone had stopped the Eskimo mother in the middle of her sewing. "What could it have been?" Labelle wondered to himself.

Labelle walked down to the lake. Perhaps the villagers had gone on an unexpected hunt. Three kayaks lay on the beach. One of them belonged to the village's chief. Wherever they had gone, the villagers had not gone by boat.

As the tale is usually told, Joe went to get help from the Mounted Police. The Moun-

Joe Labelle went to a Mounted Police station similar to this one.

ties had a station in Churchill. Churchill was some 500 miles away.

The Mounties searched the village thoroughly. They found the Eskimos' rifles. This meant that the Eskimos hadn't gone on a hunt. They would never go on a hunt and leave their rifles behind. After all, this was a land where polar bears were often seen. No hunter would want to meet up with a polar bear unless he were armed.

Outside the village, the searchers found three dogs. They had been tied to a tree. Of course, they had starved to death. The searchers figured that the villagers had disappeared at least two months ago. The searchers could tell that from some berries found in a pot. The berries would have ripened just about eight weeks ago. But the searchers couldn't figure out why the dogs had been left tied to the tree.

The searchers hunted for a trail of some sort. But there was none. All footprints had been covered by snow.

The searchers believed that the villagers had not planned their trip. Otherwise, they would have taken their dogs and their rifles with them. They also figured the people had run off in a great hurry. That's why they had left behind pots full of food and partly finished work. But why had they left so suddenly? And where had they gone?

In the 1930s, Mounties traveled by dogsled.

The searchers couldn't come up with any answers to these questions. They didn't even have any good guesses.

Stories of the mystery of the disappearing village appeared in magazines and books. But as it turned out, the disappearance may not be the real mystery. The stories said that the Mounties looked into the disappearance very carefully. But the Mounties say they never saw any such village.

Over the years, dozens of people have called or written to the Mounted Police asking about the village that disappeared. The Mounties carefully checked their files. They talked to people who have lived in northern Canada for many years. As far as the Mounties could tell, there never was a village of Anjikini. So if there never was a village, it couldn't disappear.

Could the Mounties be wrong? Was there a village near faroff Lake Anjikini that disappeared? If there wasn't, how did the story of the disappearance get started? And if it's just a story, why do magazines and books keep on printing it as though it really happened?

INDEX

95

THOMAS G. GUNNING holds a doctorate in the Psychology of Reading from Temple University in Philadelphia and is currently an associate professor in the Reading Department of Southern Connecticut State University. He has been a high school and junior high school English and reading teacher, an English department chairperson, and an elementary school reading consultant.

Dr. Gunning is the author of *Unexplained Mysteries* and *Amazing Escapes*, both of which were selected for the YASD/ALA High Interest/Low Reading Level Booklist. He is also coauthor of *New Directions in Reading*, a series of textbooks for underachieving older students, and has written a number of reading kits, reading comprehension workbooks, and articles on the teaching of reading.

Thomas G. Gunning makes his home in Newington, Connecticut, with his wife, Joan, and his children, Joy, Tim, and Faith. His oldest son, Tom, is an attorney in Massachusetts.